Bramble and Berry

The fox cub peered nervously through the long grass. He stared at the kitten's dark, striped face and her long white whiskers. He had been watching her for a while. She looked very fierce, especially when she had pounced on that piece of straw. *Please don't pounce on me, too*, the cub thought, trembling with fear. . . .

Bramble and Berry

Best▾Friends

Bramble and Berry

by Jenny Dale

Illustrated by Susan Hellard

SCHOLASTIC INC.

New York   Toronto   London   Auckland   Sydney
Mexico City   New Delhi   Hong Kong   Buenos Aires

Special thanks to Jill Atkins

ISBN 0-439-66992-8

Text copyright © 2002 by Working Partners Limited.
Illustrations copyright © 2002 by Susan Hellard.

12 11 10 9 8 7 6 5 4   6 7 8 9/0

Printed in the U.S.A.   40
First Scholastic printing, November 2004

chapter one

"Look at me!" Bramble dug her sharp claws into the wooden beam, high up in the barn. She peered down at her mom, Tabitha.

"Bramble, come down here right now," mewed Tabitha. "You'll fall!"

"But it's fun up here, Mom," the kitten meowed. "I can see all kinds of exciting things!" She loved looking up at the birds' nests high in the eaves. And she could even see mice scurrying among the bales of straw far below.

"It's all right, Mom," she purred. "I'm safe."

At that moment, Bramble felt her paws slipping. She tried to dig her claws deeper into the wooden beam. Too late! "Oops!" she wailed as she fell.

The air whistled through Bramble's whiskers and ruffled her furry coat. Halfway down, Bramble flipped her body the right way up and landed paws first in a deep pile of straw.

Tabitha trotted over to her. "You have to be more careful," she meowed, giving Bramble a lick. "You'll get into real trouble one day."

Bramble loved the feel of her mom's rough tongue rasping over her face. "Don't worry about me," she purred. She lifted her head so Tabitha could reach under her chin.

When Tabitha had finished, Bramble leaped up and scampered out into the farmyard. It was a breezy day. A piece of straw blew along the ground in front of her. Bramble pounced on it, feeling it crackle under her front paws.

A sharp gust of wind blew the straw just out of reach. It fluttered away across the yard.

"Come back here," Bramble hissed, bounding after it.

Suddenly, she stopped. A pair of dark, shiny eyes stared at her from the long grass at the edge of the yard.

Bramble crept a little nearer. She saw a thin red face, a shiny black nose, and two very pointed ears.

It was a fox!

Bramble stood still for a moment. She remembered what her mom had taught her. "Foxes are very dangerous. You must run away if you ever see one."

Shaking all over, Bramble began to

back away slowly. She hoped the fox
would not come after her.

The fox cub peered nervously through
the long grass. He stared at the kitten's
dark, striped face and her long white
whiskers. He had been watching her for a
while. She looked very fierce, especially
when she had pounced on that piece of

straw. *Please don't pounce on me, too*, the cub thought, trembling with fear.

Bramble noticed the grass quivering. The fox was shivering. "Is he frightened of *me*?" she wondered. Bramble narrowed her eyes and took a closer look. "He's very small," she meowed. "I'm not scared of *him*!"

Feeling quite brave, she stepped forward, arched her back, and hissed loudly. "Go away, fox!" she spat.

"Help!" whined the cub. In a panic, he dashed out of the long grass, past the kitten and across the farmyard.

Bramble saw a flash of red fur as the tiny fox shot by. Then she blinked. The fox had disappeared. "I frightened a fox!" she meowed in surprise.

Bramble scampered to the farmhouse. She stood on her hind legs and pushed her head through the cat flap. "Mom!" she mewed. "I frightened a fox. I scared it away!"

"A fox?" meowed Tabitha anxiously, hurrying toward her. "Are you all right?"

"Oh, yes," Bramble purred proudly. "We won't see him around here again!"

The fox cub headed for the barn. It was gloomy inside, but he could see a pile of straw in one corner. It would be a good place to hide. He dove into the straw and lay there, panting and shaking.

There were strange noises all around him, rustling and fluttering. His heart thumped. He huddled down in the straw, hoping that his mom would come and find him very soon.

Suddenly, the fox cub heard another sound. From his hiding place, he saw a boy enter the barn and walk toward the pile of straw.

"Hey!" said the boy. "There's something hiding in here."

The little fox whined. He pushed his nose deeper into the straw and closed his eyes, hoping the boy wouldn't come any closer. But then he felt a hand stroking his back.

"I don't believe it!" said the boy. "It's a fox cub."

The cub felt the boy's hands lifting him up. He was too frightened to struggle. "Help!" he whimpered.

"You poor thing," said the boy kindly. "Are you lost? Don't worry, I'll take care of you. I'd better bring you inside."

The boy's quiet voice comforted the fox. He didn't feel quite so scared when the boy carried him out of the barn.

A woman was standing near the farmhouse door. "Hi, Mark," she called. "What do you have there?"

"A fox cub," the boy replied. "May I keep him?"

The woman hurried over. "He's very tiny," she said. "He'll need a lot of care until we find his mom." She took the cub and petted him.

The fox cub was not shaking quite so much now. These people had gentle hands and voices. Maybe they would take him

back to his mom. He snuggled into the
woman's sweater as she carried him into
the farmhouse. Then he pricked up his
ears and looked around, his eyes wide. He
was in a big room, and it was cool and
quiet after the hot, dusty farmyard.

The woman put the fox down on a soft

blanket. She filled a bowl with water and put it beside him. The cub looked at the water. He was really thirsty. Slowly, he crept forward to the bowl and began to drink.

Bramble was happily munching some crunchy dry food when Mark and Mrs. Gates came in. Out of the corner of her eye, she spotted a bushy red tail. She stopped eating and watched the fox cub drink some water.

"What's *he* doing in here?" she hissed. "I thought I got rid of him."

"I think I'll call him Berry," she heard Mark say.

"Berry is a good name for him," said Mrs. Gates. "His fur is the right color."

Bramble jumped up. "I'm going to frighten that fox away again!" she meowed. She began to gallop across the kitchen.

Berry saw the stripe-faced creature racing toward him. "Oh, no!" he whined. "Here comes that cat again!"

chapter two

"What are you doing here?" Bramble hissed. She arched her back.

Berry pressed his nose into the blanket. "Please don't hurt me," he whined.

Bramble felt confused as she looked at the trembling fox. She didn't know what her mom was making such a fuss about. Foxes weren't scary at all!

Tabitha came and stood behind Bramble. "Well!" she meowed. "So this is the fox you frightened away!"

"Yes, Mom," Bramble purred proudly.

"I hadn't realized it was so small," mewed Tabitha.

Bramble rubbed her head against her mom's face. "Aren't all foxes like this?" she asked.

"Oh, no," Tabitha replied. "Grown-up foxes are much bigger. This is only a very young cub. No wonder he's scared."

Berry wanted to hide from the stripe-faced kitten. And there was an even *bigger* cat with her. He tugged at the blanket and tried to wriggle underneath it. The edge of the blanket twitched. In a flash, the kitten pounced on it and began to drag the blanket off him.

Berry growled, "Let go!" He grabbed the other end between his teeth and pulled. The more Berry pulled at one

end, the harder the kitten tugged at the other.

Finally, Berry gave up. He lay still, panting heavily, his heart pounding in his chest. "I want my mom," he whimpered sadly.

The kitten came and sat down beside him. "Why don't you want to play with me?" she meowed.

At that moment, the woman hurried over and petted the kitten gently. "Now, Bramble, you fierce little monster," she said. "Leave our visitor alone."

The kitten purred and rubbed her head against the woman's hand. Then she trotted away.

Berry sniffed and sat up. What was that delicious smell? He crouched down as the boy loomed over him and put a dish on the floor. Berry sniffed again. He didn't know what was in the dish, but it smelled very tasty! He stepped forward and took a mouthful. Yum! He gulped down all the food and then had another drink of water.

After that he felt much better. He crept back to the blanket and lay on his side, with his tail stretched out across the floor. He could keep an eye on the two cats from there. They were eating some food as well.

Bramble had nearly finished. She turned around to look at Berry. "You look lonely," she mewed. She quickly washed her whiskers, then jumped up and scampered across the room toward the fox cub.

Berry's heart beat faster as he watched the kitten racing toward him. What was she going to do this time? To his surprise, Bramble stopped, reached out her paw, and tapped the tip of his tail.

Berry jumped up and swished his tail behind him. "What are you doing?" he yapped angrily.

But Bramble didn't answer. Instead, she gently patted his nose. Berry blinked, then tried to pat Bramble back. But she dodged away and raced across the kitchen.

"Come back!" Berry called.

"I bet you can't catch me!" meowed Bramble playfully.

Berry set off after Bramble. He tried to

catch up with her as she scampered under the table, but it wasn't easy. His paws skidded on the slippery floor. It wasn't like the soft ground in the woods where he lived.

Berry chased Bramble around and around the kitchen, sliding into corners and bumping into the table legs. His ears flapped madly, and his tail streamed out behind him. The faster he ran, the more excited he got. This was fun!

Suddenly, Bramble came to a stop. Berry crashed into her with a bump. They fell over and landed in a heap.

Berry looked at Bramble. She wasn't at all scary, really. She was soft and furry, and she was out of breath, just like he was.

Bramble sat up. "Phew! I'm thirsty," she mewed. "Do you want a drink?"

"Yes, I do," yapped Berry.

They trotted to the water bowl, and side by side, they began to lap the cool water.

chapter three

That night, Berry curled up on his blanket. He tried hard to get to sleep, but strange humming and clicking noises kept him awake. He missed his mom and his den in the woods, and he whimpered quietly in the darkness. Luckily, he could hear Bramble and Tabitha purring. It made him feel better to know that Bramble was nearby. She might even help him find his mom in the morning. Berry started to feel sleepy at last.

As soon as it was light, Bramble leaped

over the side of her basket and bounded across the kitchen floor. "Hey, Berry!" she mewed as she skidded to a halt in front of the blanket. "Are you awake?"

There was no reply, so Bramble craned her neck over the edge of the blanket. She saw a bundle of red fur, two pointed ears, and a nose tucked under a white-tipped tail. Berry was fast asleep.

"Come on, you lazybones!" Bramble meowed, more loudly. "I'm ready to play."

Berry blinked and sat up, looking at Bramble with his head turned to one side. He yawned. He didn't really feel like playing yet. He still felt very sleepy.

Bramble leaped onto the blanket, then bounced off again and raced across the floor, but Berry didn't move. Bramble

scampered back and began tugging a
corner of the blanket. "It's time to play,"
she meowed.

Berry slowly stood up and stretched. He
watched as Bramble scampered over to
a little yellow ball. She tapped it so it
rolled toward Berry, then chased it and
tapped it once again. The ball rolled
temptingly across the smooth floor.

Berry bounded off the blanket and raced after the ball. He snatched it up in his mouth. Then he shook his head, and the ball flew into the air. But as he ran after it again, he felt Bramble's paws grab him. He tumbled onto his side with a grunt.

Bramble pounced on him, and they rolled over and over together on the kitchen floor. She could feel Berry's tickly fur under her paws. She playfully batted his ears, keeping her claws tucked in. "I told you I was going to cheer you up," she panted. "Come on. I'll show you what else we can do."

The door to the living room was open. Bramble squeezed through the gap and boldly trotted over to the curtains.

"Watch this!" she mewed, digging her claws into the thick, soft material. Up and up she climbed, until Berry looked like a tiny ball of red fluff far below. Suddenly, the door opened, and Mrs. Gates and Mark came in.

"Bramble!" cried Mrs. Gates as she lifted the kitten down. "You'll ruin my curtains, you bad girl."

But Bramble was too excited to listen. She wriggled and jumped out of Mrs. Gates's arms. As soon as her paws touched the carpet, she raced off with Berry close behind her. There was a warm, thick rug on the other side of the room. It had fluffy tassels on one end. Bramble loved playing with them. She sprang onto the tassels and pulled.

Berry crouched next to her and tugged a tassel with his teeth.

"Bramble!" called Mark, laughing and clapping his hands. "Don't teach Berry all your naughty tricks." He shooed them away from the rug, back into the kitchen.

As soon as Berry entered the room, he smelled something delicious. Food! He lifted his nose and sniffed the air. The yummy smell was coming from something on the table. Berry thought for a moment. If he could just pull that cloth off the table, the food might fall onto the floor beside him. He reached up and held the edge of the tablecloth in his mouth.

"Stop!" shouted Mark, grabbing the cloth.

Berry let go and dove under the table, where Bramble was waiting for him.

"Too bad," Bramble mewed, nudging him with her head. Then she heard a familiar rattling sound. "Don't worry, Berry," she meowed. "I can hear Mark getting my breakfast ready. Crunchy dry food — yum! We can share."

After breakfast, Bramble and Berry curled up together on Berry's blanket and had a nap. Berry woke up first. He had been asleep for hours, and now he felt full of energy. He jumped up and trotted over to the door. There was a little square flap in it that he hadn't noticed before.

Berry pressed his nose up against the

flap and felt his tummy flip over with excitement. He could smell damp grass and leafy trees. The woods! He butted the flap with his head. It swung open, and Berry caught a glimpse of the farmyard through the little gap.

"Bramble, wake up!" he yapped.

Bramble uncurled and sat up. "What's the matter, Berry?" she mewed sleepily.

"I've found a little door," Berry barked. "I think it leads outside."

"That's my cat flap," Bramble mewed. "Watch." She ran over to Berry. Then she stood on her hind legs and pushed her nose against the swinging door. As it opened, she wriggled through the hole. The last thing Berry saw was a flick of her fluffy tail. Then she was gone.

Suddenly, the cat flap swung toward Berry, and Bramble's face reappeared. "Come on," she meowed. "It's easy." Then she disappeared again.

Berry nervously touched the flap with his nose.

"Hurry up!" called Bramble from the other side of the door.

Berry didn't find it very easy at all. He pushed and wriggled and scrambled with his back paws. The sides of the little doorway brushed against his fur. At last, he slithered out into the farmyard. But the flap swung back down and hit him on the bottom!

"Ouch!" he yelped, jumping to his paws. Then he stopped. What was that loud roaring noise? Berry flattened his ears and looked around wildly.

Just then, a big red thing thundered into the farmyard, making the loudest noise Berry had ever heard.

chapter four

Bramble watched as Berry shot like an arrow back through the cat flap. She bounded after him and found him huddled in his blanket. He was trembling from the end of his nose to the tip of his bushy tail.

Bramble licked his fur. "What's the matter?" she purred in surprise.

"Th-that red thing," Berry whimpered. "It s-scared me."

"It's only a tractor!" Bramble meowed. How could Berry be scared of a silly old tractor?

"W-what's a t-t-tractor?" Berry yelped.

"Mr. Gates uses it to ride all over the farm," Bramble explained. "It won't hurt you. Come on."

Berry's paws were still shaking when he left his comfy blanket and followed Bramble through the cat flap again. It was easier to get through this time. Berry was very glad to see that the red tractor was chugging out of the gate.

"This way," meowed Bramble as she scampered across the farmyard.

Berry followed close behind her. She led him under the fence and into a wide green field. Berry felt a cool shiver of excitement down his back. He had been in this field before. On the far side were some trees.

Berry paused and sniffed. He knew where he was! Those trees were at the edge of the woods where he used to live. Maybe his mom was somewhere in there. He hurtled past Bramble and dashed across the field toward the trees.

"Wait for me!" Bramble called, but Berry was in too much of a hurry.

Suddenly, a brightly colored butterfly fluttered past his nose, tickling him with its velvety wings. Berry leaped up and tried to catch it, but it flew away. A sweet smell filled his nose. He looked down at his paws and saw lots of little flowers all around him. He burrowed his nose into the flowers and rolled in the grass. The sun made his fur glow warmly, and a gentle breeze ruffled his ears. It was great to be outside again!

Just then, he heard Mark calling. "Bramble! Berry! Where are you? It's supper time!"

"Yum!" Berry yapped. "I'm hungry." He began to trot back across the field. He looked around for Bramble, but he didn't see her anywhere.

Meanwhile, Bramble had been chasing a baby rabbit. She had followed it right to the edge of the field before the rabbit disappeared down a hole. Bramble looked around and realized she was very close to the woods. She could smell lots of exciting scents coming from the trees. "This might be a good place to explore," she mewed, trotting nearer.

She stopped at the edge of the woods and peered through the thick green leaves. It looked dark under the trees, but Bramble didn't mind. She felt very brave. With her whiskers twitching and ears pricked, she stepped under the fence and into the woods.

A big black beetle scuttled across her path. It was smooth and shiny. Bramble reached out to touch it, but it slid under a leaf and disappeared out of sight.

Something tickled her head. Bramble looked up. A spider was hanging from its fine thread just above her. The tiny creature swung to and fro in the breeze.

Bramble was just about to reach up when she heard a strange snuffling sound behind her. She whipped around and pounced.

"Ouch!" she yowled, springing away from the prickly thing. She watched, her eyes very wide, as the spiky ball slowly uncurled. A pointed black nose and two tiny black eyes appeared from the middle of the prickles. Then the strange animal shuffled off into the bushes.

Bramble shook her tingling paws and

decided not to chase after it. She walked
farther into the woods. A cold breeze ruffled her fur, and she shivered. It was
starting to get dark. Perhaps it wasn't
such a good idea to come into the woods
on her own.

"I'd better go back to the farm now,"
she meowed to herself.

But which way was home? Bramble
couldn't remember. She peered around,

43

but all the trees looked the same. Never mind. She would soon find the way.

Bramble squeezed between two large bushes, but she couldn't go any farther because there was a very tall tree in the way. She backed out of the bushes and tried another path. It led straight into a clump of prickly shrubs.

Suddenly, a scary hooting sound came from high up in the trees. "Whooo are you?"

Bramble jumped and peered up into the darkness. She couldn't see a thing.

"Whooo?"

What was making that creepy sound? Bramble narrowed her eyes, but she could only see shadowy branches swaying in the wind.

Bramble realized she was lost. She crawled under a bush with thick green leaves and thought about home. She began to yowl loudly. "Mom! Berry! Help!"

chapter five

It was warm and cozy in the kitchen. Berry munched on the dry food that Mark had put in his bowl. When he had finished, he licked every last crumb from around his mouth and nose. Then he looked at Bramble's bowl, which was next to his. It was still full. Where had Bramble gone? She should have come back by now.

Berry trotted to the cat flap and looked through it. It was nearly dark outside. "Bramble!" he yapped. "Where are you?"

Berry was ready for a nap on his blanket, but he couldn't settle down while he was worried about his friend. He had to go and find Bramble. Berry jumped through the cat flap, ran across the farmyard, and peered through the fence. He couldn't see Bramble anywhere.

Berry walked into the field and stared at the woods. The sound of the wind in the leaves made him feel safe. But Berry knew it would be a dangerous place for a kitten at night.

"Oh, Bramble!" he whined. "Where have you gone?" He trotted across the field. "Bramble!" he called a bit louder. "Can you hear me?" He stopped to listen, but there was no answer. "I'll have to go into the woods to look for her," he yapped.

As he stepped under the trees, Berry lifted his nose and sniffed the familiar woodland smells. A cool, gentle breeze smoothed his fur. He was home!

"Whooo?" came a call from above his head.

Berry looked up. "Hello, owl!" he barked. "I'm home!"

✣ ✣ ✣

Deep in the woods, Bramble huddled in her hiding place under the bush. She was feeling scared. The noises of the night seemed to close in around her, rustling and hissing and hooting.

Suddenly, she heard a loud bark not far away. Bramble jumped. Her tail fluffed up, and she opened her eyes wide. What if that was a *grown-up* fox? Now Bramble didn't feel brave at all.

"Help!" she yowled. "I want to go home!"

Berry pricked up his ears. He could hear a faint cry in the distance. "Bramble!" he yapped as loudly as he could. "Is that you?"

Bramble held her breath and peered into the shadows. They were full of dark, spooky shapes. Something brushed against her back. She whipped around, but it was only a branch. She pricked up her ears, straining to hear the loud bark again. But all she could hear was a tiny yapping sound. It didn't sound scary. It sounded very familiar.

Bramble sat up. "Berry!" she meowed at the top of her voice. "I'm here! Help!"

Berry heard Bramble's cry very clearly. "Hooray!" he yapped. "I've found her!" He bounded through the bushes toward the sound. "Don't be afraid, Bramble," he barked bravely into the dark woods. "I'm coming!"

chapter six

Bramble sat up straight. Berry had come to rescue her! She leaped out from under the bush. "Berry!" she yowled. "I'm over here!"

Suddenly, Berry came bounding into the clearing from behind a tree. His fur gleamed like silver in the moonlight. He galloped toward her with his tail stretched out behind him.

Bramble raced over to him on shaky paws. "Thank goodness you found me," she purred, burying her nose in his thick fur. "It's so scary in here!"

"Don't worry," Berry yapped, licking his friend's ear. "I've come to take you home. Let's go." He turned and set off through the woods. After a few steps, he stopped and looked around. Bramble was so close behind, she bumped into his tail. Her eyes were very wide, and her fur was fluffed up. Berry felt sorry for his friend. *The woods must seem very spooky to her*, he thought.

Bramble kept as close to Berry as she could as they trotted through the woods. She couldn't wait to get home. "Thank you for coming to find me," she mewed. "I was really scared."

Suddenly, a dark, slinky shape stepped out onto the path. Bramble saw a long,

narrow face and two bright black eyes.
Sharp white teeth glinted in the darkness.

Bramble stopped. Then she arched her
back and spat. "Berry," she hissed. "Look
out!"

Berry looked up. But he didn't seem
scared at all. Instead, he let out a cry
of delight. "Mom!" he yapped, leaping

up and licking the animal's face. "Where have you been?"

"Everywhere," barked Berry's mother. She gently nuzzled him with her nose. "I've been looking all over the woods for you. I thought I'd *never* find you."

Berry felt bubbles of happiness fizzing inside him. He had come into the woods to rescue Bramble, and now he had found his mom, too! He pushed his nose into his mother's warm fur and smelled her familiar scent. "I've missed you, Mom," he mumbled.

Bramble watched Berry and his mom making a fuss over each other. She could feel her fur bristling on the back of her neck. It was scary being this close to a grown-up fox! Her teeth looked very

sharp, and she was much, much bigger than Bramble, or even Bramble's mom. Bramble inched backward under a bush.

"Hey, Bramble," yapped Berry, hurrying toward her. "Why are you hiding? There's nothing to be scared of."

Bramble crept slowly forward, keeping her eyes on the big fox's face.

Berry's mom stared down at her. "Who's this?" she asked.

"It's Bramble," yapped Berry.

Bramble took a deep breath. Her heart was hammering so loudly, she thought Berry's mom must be able to hear it. "Hello," she mewed.

Berry ran over to Bramble and pressed his body against her fur. "Bramble took care of me," he explained to his mom. "She cheered me up when I was lost, and she played with me, and now we're best friends."

"Thank you, Bramble," Berry's mom barked kindly. "But what are you doing in the woods at night?"

Bramble went a few steps nearer. "I was

exploring," she meowed. "But I got lost. Berry came to find me."

"And now I'm taking her back to the farm," yapped Berry.

His mom frowned. "We should stay in the woods," she barked. "It's safer for us in here."

"But we have to take her to the fence on the other side of the field," Berry protested. He wanted to make sure that Bramble got safely back to *her* mom, now that he had found his.

"All right," replied his mom. "But we must be careful."

Berry and his mom set off through the dark woods, following an invisible path between the bushes. Bramble trotted behind them. They soon reached the edge of the trees. Across the field, the lights from the farmhouse twinkled in the darkness. Bramble sighed happily. She couldn't wait to see her mom again, and the warm, cozy kitchen. *And* she hadn't had any supper!

She dashed out of the trees and across

the field, with Berry and his mom racing beside her.

When they had almost reached the farm, Berry's mom stopped. "Stay here, son," she barked quietly. "We mustn't go any farther."

Bramble and Berry banged into each other as they skidded to a halt. They rolled over and over in the long, wet grass.

Berry rubbed his silky red head against Bramble's soft kitten fur. "But, Mom!" he whined, sitting up. "I'll miss Bramble."

"I'll miss you, too," Bramble purred. Just then, she smelled the straw from the barn and heard the chickens clucking in the yard. "But I do want to go home!" she added.

"It's time for us to go," barked Berry's mom.

Bramble nuzzled her cheek against Berry's pointed face. "Will you come and visit me again soon?" she purred sadly.

"Yes, lots," Berry promised. "But I can't come into the farmyard anymore. It's not safe for foxes."

"And I'd better not go into the woods again!" mewed Bramble. "It's scary in there!"

"But we could meet in this field," Berry yapped.

"Okay!" Bramble purred. "That's a good idea."

Berry and his mom turned toward the woods, their long tails swishing against the grass.

Bramble felt sad as she watched them slip away into the night. She would miss Berry very much, but she was really glad he had found his mom.

"See you soon!" she called as the white tip of Berry's tail disappeared into the darkness. Then she jumped through the fence and ran toward the farmhouse.